Always Carry Me With You

For Téa.
For Zoé.
So that they always remember.
H.É.

To Gwen. My lucky charm.
F.B.

Hervé would like to thank Fred Benaglia for his talent.
Aude Sarrazin for her enthusiasm.
And Shelly Reinstein for the memory of Flagstaff, AZ.

First published as *Au Fond de ta Poche* in 2022 by Éditions Glénat, in Grenoble, France.

First published in the UK in 2024 by Ivy Kids, an imprint of The Quarto Group.
1 Triptych Place, London, SE1 9SH, United Kingdom
T (0)20 7700 6700 F (0)20 7700 8066 www.Quarto.com

Translated from the original French by Hannah Dove.

A catalogue record for this book is available from the British Library.

ISBN 978-0-7112-9512-4
eBook ISBN 978-0-7112-9515-5

Set in Austral Sans

Commissioning Editor: Hannah Dove
Production Controller: Dawn Cameron
Publisher: Georgia Buckthorn

Manufactured in the UK by Halstan & Co. Ltd. on recycled FSC paper. HA022024
Printed by a company certified to ISO 14001: 2015
and carbon balanced in association with the World Land Trust.

9 8 7 6 5 4 3 2 1

Always Carry Me With You

WRITTEN BY
HERVÉ ÉPARVIER

ILLUSTRATED BY
FRED BENAGLIA

I wish I were a stone.

Stones are beautiful.
Stones live many lives.

A stone doesn't need anything to be happy.
It just *is* and that's all.

Stones are useful.
We use them to build houses.

The pyramids in Egypt and the great palaces and castles of the world are built from stone.

Statues by great artists and towering skyscrapers are made from stone too.

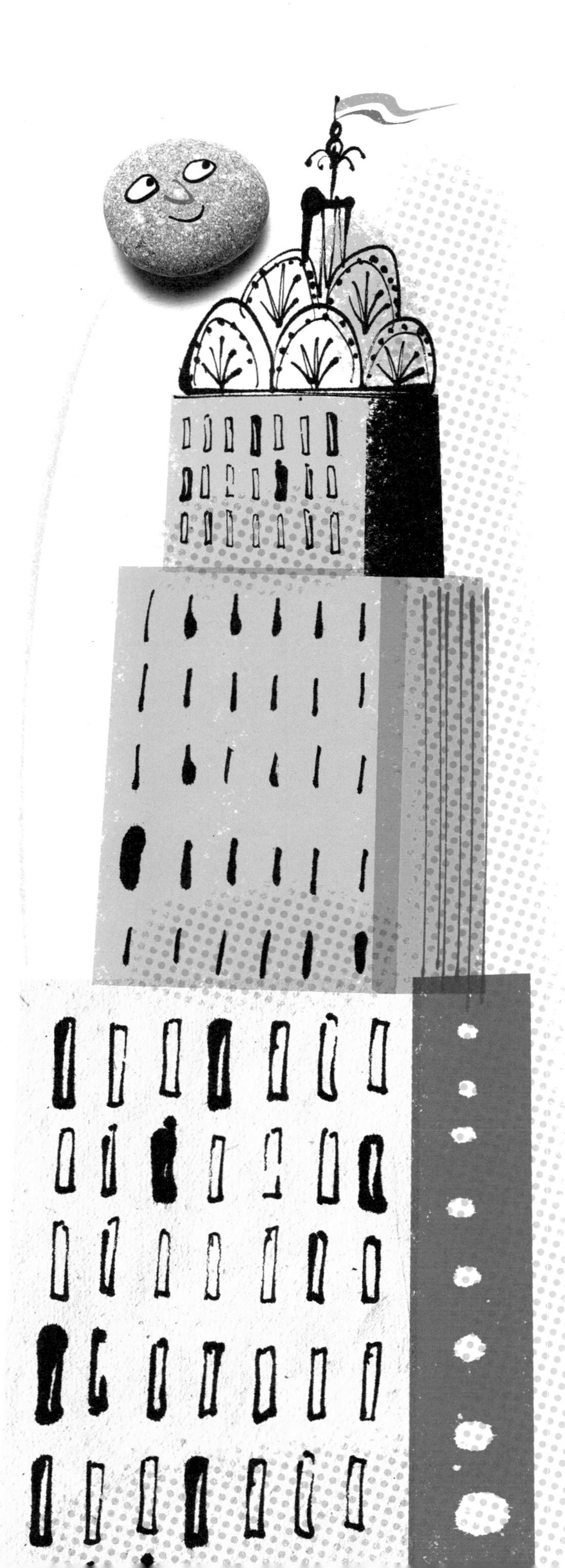

Stones are fun.

Stones can skim across water,
tap gently on a friend's window or
lead us in a game of hopscotch.

And when two stones collide,
with a little luck, they make a spark
and start a blazing fire!

Fire that can keep us warm
(or even toast a marshmallow).

If a stone is very handsome,
it can spend its life
on a plinth.

Somewhere in a museum,
perhaps, or given pride
of place on a shelf, to be
admired and treasured.

When a stone is big
– really, EXTRA big –
the top might get covered in snow.
So much that people can slip and slide
right down it, on sledges, on skis
or just on their bums!

Whoosh!

And when a stone is small
– really, extra small –
it can become all round and soft,
and brush gently beneath our feet as
we walk along the beach.

It feels glorious.

Stones can be found anywhere
but some come from far away. From the
Moon, or even further out in space.

Scientists can study stones with microscopes
to learn all sorts of wonderful secrets.

Stones are FULL of information.

Yes, I wish I were a stone.

A little stone pebble.

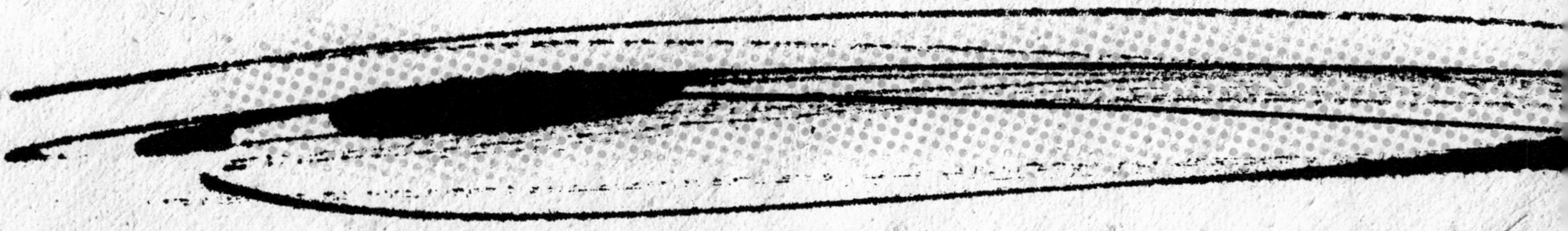

A pebble that would fit snugly in your
pocket, between a tissue and a sweet.

A pebble that you wouldn't always notice
but that would always be with you.

A pebble to keep you company,
to comfort you on days when
you feel afraid and to remind
you that you are not alone.

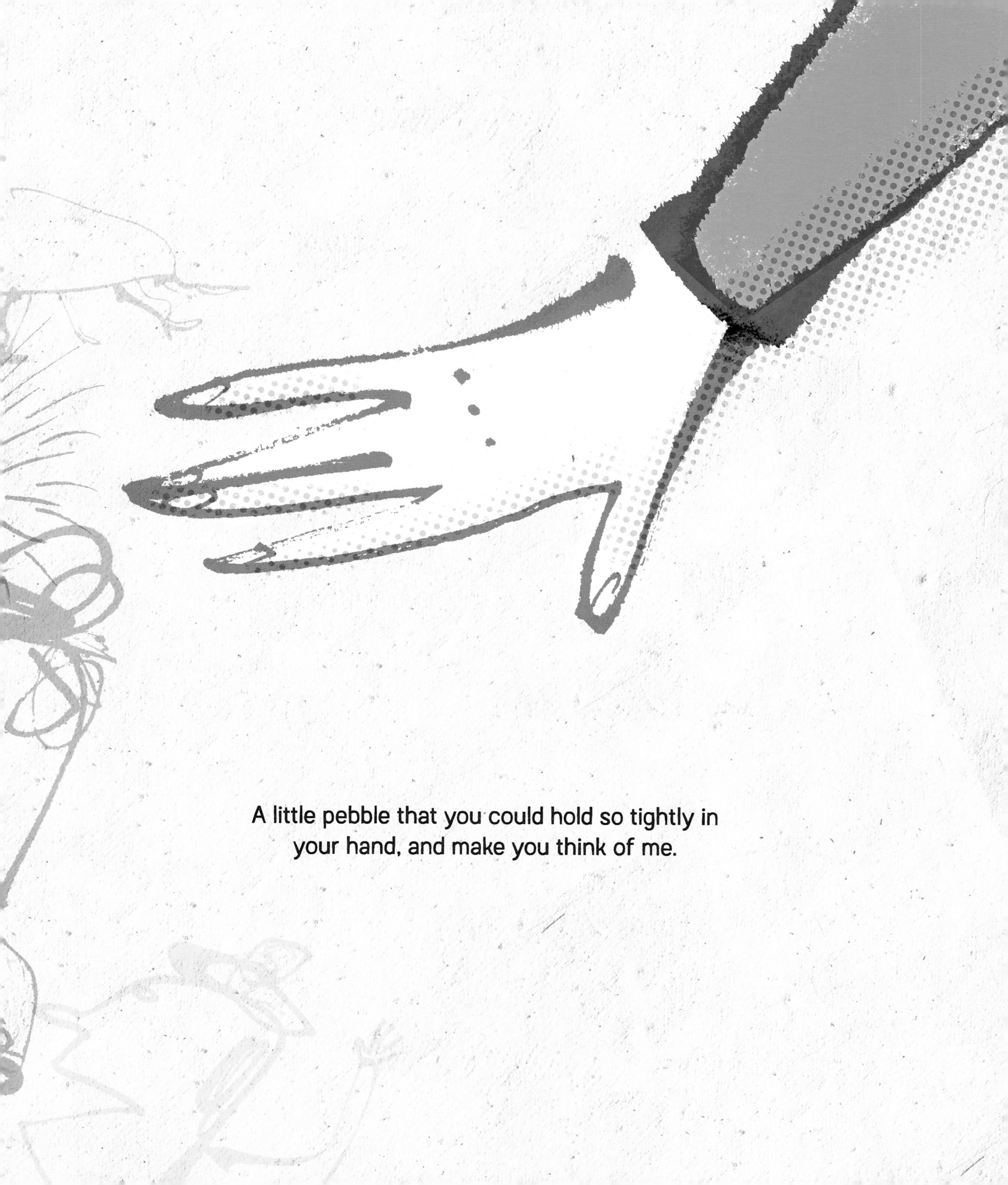

A little pebble that you could hold so tightly in
your hand, and make you think of me.

Yes.
I wish I were a little stone pebble at the
bottom of your pocket so you could
always carry me with you . . .

. . . and remember that I love you.